# KINDERGARTEN KIDS

## RIDDLES, REBUSES, WIGGLES, GIGGLES, AND MORE!

original rhymes by **Stephanie Calmenson**

pictures by **Melissa Sweet**

HarperCollins*Publishers*

To our readers

—S.C. and M.S.

Kindergarten Kids
Text copyright © 2005 by Stephanie Calmenson
Illustrations copyright © 2005 by Melissa Sweet
Manufactured in China.
All rights reserved.
www.harperchildrens.com
Library of Congress Cataloging-in-Publication Data
Calmenson, Stephanie.
Kindergarten kids : riddles, rebuses, wiggles, giggles, and more! / original rhymes
by Stephanie Calmenson ; pictures by Melissa Sweet.—1st ed.
p.   cm.
ISBN 0-06-000713-3 — ISBN 0-06-000714-1 (lib. bdg.)
1. Kindergarten—Juvenile poetry. 2. Children's poetry, American.  I. Sweet, Melissa.
II. Title.
PS3553.A425K56 2005     811'.54—dc22
2004004175     CIP
AC
Typography by Stephanie Bart-Horvath
1 2 3 4 5 6 7 8 9 10
❖
First Edition

# Contents

Good Morning! 4

Show-and-Tell 6

Mr. Wig, Our Guinea Pig 8

Puzzled 10

Popcorn Hop 12

Loose Tooth 13

Pizza Party 14

Oops! 16

Wiggle and Wag 18

Boo! It's Halloween! 20

Quiet, Please! 22

Open a Book 23

Letter Hunt 24

Thanksgiving 25

Do Skunks Send Stinky Valentine Cards? 26

One Hundred Words Are in This Poem 28

See You Later, Alligator! 30

Kindergarten Kids 32

# Good Morning!
## How are you today?

Good morning!
Who's sleepy?
Who's sniffly?
Who's jumpy?
Who's grumpy?
Who's silly?

Who's happy?
Who's listening?
Who's ready to learn?
Who's ready to play?
Who's ready to start
Our kindergarten day?

BRAD

JAMAL

ANNA

MICHAEL

SUE

# Show-and-Tell
## What will you bring?

Look what I built.
It really does float.
It's blue with white sails.
Do you like my toy _____?

I go to the beach
In all kinds of weather.
Here's a treasure I found.
It's a seagull _____!

Who likes dogs?
If you do, take a look.
There are pictures on the pages
In my new _____!

I mix, pour, and measure
When Dad and I bake.
I put icing on, too.
Who wants a _____?

# Mr. Wig, Our Guinea Pig

## Where is Mr. Wig going?

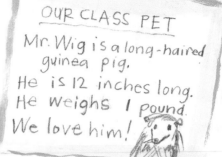

OUR CLASS PET

Mr. Wig is a long-haired guinea pig.
He is 12 inches long.
He weighs 1 pound.
We love him!

Mr. Wig, our guinea pig,
Surprised us yesterday.
We were cleaning out his cage
When he somehow got away.

Quick! Is he under the easel?
Is he hiding behind the blocks?
Is he on our teacher's desk?
Is he in our collection of rocks?

Math Corner

1 2 3
4 5 6
7 8 9
  10

Do you see him in the math corner,
Or in the library under a book?
Is he napping in our playhouse?
Where, oh, where do we look?

Hush, everyone, listen.
Do you hear that squeaking noise?
It's coming from the play corner.
Look who's under those _____!

One
Little
Monkey

# Puzzled

Do you just want to quit sometimes?

Too hard! Too hard!
These pieces don't fit.
I'm puzzled by this puzzle.
I really want to quit.

"Don't give up," I tell myself.
"Keep trying. You'll do fine.
Look for all the clues you can—
Color, story, shape, size, line."

I take a breath. I look again.
Colors match. I see a square.
The pieces fit together.
They go there and there and there!

So easy! So easy!
I did it! Puzzle's done.
I'm ready for another.
I want a *harder* one.

# Popcorn Hop

### Everybody do
### the popcorn dance!

Put your popcorn
   in a pot.
Wait till it gets
   really hot.

When you start to
   feel the heat,
Listen for the
   popcorn beat:

Pop-pop-POP-pop
   pop-pop-POP!
Come and do the
   popcorn hop!

Cooking Center

# Loose Tooth

**Look who's got a new smile.**

My tooth is wobbling.
It's wiggling while I'm
Talking and giggling.
It's wiggling. It's wobbling.
It's snack time. I'm gobbling.
It's looser. No doubt.
It's wiggling. It's *out!*
Look at me! Hooray!
My tooth fell out today!

13

# Pizza Party

There's a party in the
math corner.
You're invited!

Square box.
Round pie.
Triangle slices.
I'm not shy . . .

I'll take a slice.
I bet it's great.
How many slices?
I count eight.

Two pies.
Eight plus eight.
Sixteen slices.
Pizza's great.

Crusty, saucy,
Stringy, cheesy,
Tasty pizza
Sure does please me!

9 10 11 12 13 14 15 16

# Oops!

**Don't worry.
*Everyone* makes mistakes!**

Anna dropped some crayons.
She broke her favorite blue.
Jamal was counting cups for juice.
Oops! He left out two.

Michael overwatered
Our avocado tree.
Now it's brown and droopy
Where green leaves used to be.

Our music teacher missed a note.
He played a silly tune.
Our principal said, "Good morning,"
When it was afternoon.

Oops, oops, oops again.
Oh, for goodness' sakes!
Don't feel bad, remember:
*Everyone* makes mistakes!

# Wiggle and Wag

**Can you wiggle? Can you wag?
Let's see!**

I've got a puppy tail.
I wag it
Left and right.
What a sight!

I've got big bird wings.
I flap them
Up and down.
Good-bye, ground!

I've got a turtle neck.
I stretch it
To and fro.
Watch me go.

I've got pony legs.
I gallop
Far and wide.
Come for a ride.

I've got monkey hands.
I wave them
In the air.
Hello, out there!

I've got my very own body.
I wiggle, wiggle, wiggle, wiggle,
Wiggle, wiggle, wiggle, wiggle,
Wiggle, wiggle, wiggle, wiggle it.
Then I sit!

# Boo! It's Halloween!
## Look who's on parade.

Zoom, zoom, zoom!
I fly on my broom
With my pointy black hat
And my black-as-night cat.
*Who am I?*

Here I stand all alone,
Nothing but bone
After bone
After bone.
*Who am I?*

On Halloween night
I'm dressed in white.
Beware. I scare.
"BOO!" Did I frighten you?
*Who am I?*

I'm orange and round. Now I just need a face.
Wherever you put it will be a good place.
Make it silly or scary. Either is fun.
Draw it on. Cut it out. Thank you. I'm done!
*Who am I?*

# Quiet, Please!

**Being quiet isn't easy, is it?**

Gab, gab.
Giggle, giggle.
Psst, psst.
Wiggle, wiggle.

Cough, sigh.
Hiccup, sneeze.
Teacher asks,
"Quiet, please!"

One more giggle.
One more sneeze.
Eyes on your teacher.
Quiet, please!

# Open a Book

**It's showtime!**
**Pick up a book and read.**

Open a book
And turn a page.
A world opens up
Just like a stage.

The words are performers.
Their show's just for you.
You'll laugh, cry,
Learn something new.

You have a front-row seat.
So go on, turn a page!
A world opens up
Just like a stage.

# Letter Hunt

**Can you find all twenty-six letters
of the alphabet?**

On the blackboard do you see
The letters a, b, c, d, e, f, g?
Can you find chicks and a mother hen?
They're hiding h, i, j, k, l, m, n.
Tumbled blocks make a great big mess.
Where are o, p, q, r, and s?
There are lots of letters in our library.
Do you see t, u, v, w, x, y, z?
Did you find the letters? Did you have fun?
The letter hunt's over. Job well done!

# Thanksgiving

## What are *you* thankful for?

My teacher says, "Name ten things you're thankful for."
I say, "I'm thankful for Mommy, Daddy, my new rubber dinosaur.

"I'm thankful for my grandma, my little brother, my friends.
Look! My new dinosaur's tail bends!

"I'm thankful for my cat. His name is Boris.
Do you know this dinosaur's a stegosaurus?

"I'm thankful I'm healthy and I have enough to eat.
I love my dinosaur's scaly skin and the claws on his feet.

"I need to name one more thing I'm thankful for.
I know! I'm glad I'm not a dinosaur. I wouldn't be here anymore!"

# Do Skunks Send Valentine Cards?

**Hold your nose!**

Do skunks send
Stinky valentine cards
That say, "I hope this smells
For yards and yards"?

Would a whale's valentine
Spray up from her spout,
Spelling, "Darling, it's you
I can't live without"?

How about elephants?
Do their valentines say,
"Let's pack up our trunks
And run far away"?

Do fish in love
Drop each other a line
Saying, "I'm hooked on you.
Will you please be mine"?

How about an octopus?
Would he say, "You're grand.
I want to hold your
Hand, hand, hand, hand,
Hand, hand, hand, hand"?

If you were an animal
On Valentine's Day,
Which one would you be?
What would you say?

# One Hundred Words Are in This Poem

## Count them!

There are one hundred legs on a centipede,
One hundred crayons in a box,

One hundred buttons on our coats,
One hundred toes inside our socks,

One hundred numbers on our teacher's dress,
One hundred snails in our tank,

One hundred books in our library,
One hundred pennies in our bank,

One hundred streamers in the air,
One hundred cookies on a plate,

One hundred cupcakes for our party,
One hundred ways to celebrate.

One hundred days we've been together.
One hundred days have quickly passed.

One hundred words are in this poem.
Now you have reached the very last.

# See You Later, Alligator!
## There are lots of ways to say good-bye.

See you later, alligator.
Bye for now, mooing cow.
In a while, crocodile.
Say good-bye, butterfly.
Time to flee, bumblebee.
Come back soon, brave baboon.
Out the door, wild boar.
Here's a hug, little bug.
Leaving here, spotted deer.
Moving on, handsome swan.

Hurry up, happy pup.

No baloney, silly pony.

Gotta go, hippo.

Here's your ticket, jumpy cricket.

Bye to you, cute gnu.

Hit the road, hopping toad.

Time to float, billy goat.

Let's scram, gentle lamb.

On your way, blue jay.

**SEE YOU TOMORROW!**

# Kindergarten Kids

### Say it loud. Be proud!

We're kindergarten kids. That's who we are!

Keep your eyes on us. We're going far!
*Say it loud. We're proud!*

We try our best to get along.

We're a kindergarten family and we are strong.
*Say it loud. We're proud!*

There's a lot we do. There's a lot we know.

Keep your eyes on us. Watch us go, go, go!
*SAY IT LOUD! WE'RE PROUD!*